I Like THIS Color!

Liz Goulet Dubois

sourcebooks
jabberwocky

See how pretty this orange tiger lily is!

boop boop

Here's a pink carnation!
So perky! See?

boop boop

22

GREAT GALLOPING GECKOS!!

What do we have here?!

For Eric, who has been by my side through it all.

—LGD

Prismacolor pencils and Adobe Photoshop were used to prepare the full color art.

Published by Sourcebooks Jabberwocky, an imprint of Sourcebooks Kids
P.O. Box 4410, Naperville, Illinois 60567-4410
(630) 961-3900
sourcebookskids.com

Cataloging-in-Publication Data is on file with the Library of Congress.

Source of Production: PrintPlus, Shenzhen, Guangdong Province, China
Date of Production: October 2022
Run Number: 5027272

Printed and bound in China.
PP 10 9 8 7 6 5 4 3 2 1